HOUSE HELD UP BY TREES

*Not far from here, I have seen a house held up
by the hands of trees. This is its story.*

Ted Kooser   *illustrated by* Jon Klassen

CANDLEWICK PRESS

WHEN IT WAS NEW, the house stood alone on a bare square of earth. There was a newly planted lawn around it, but not a single tree to give shade in summer or to rattle its bare twigs in the winter cold. There had been trees there once, but all of them had been cut down to make room for the house. Even their stumps had been pulled up and burned.

But in the lots on either side, there were wild trees of all kinds—maple and elm and ash and hackberry and cottonwood, all noisy with wind and birdsong. When the wind blew toward the house in spring, the children who lived in it could smell the tiny, sweet green flowers on the trees. Beneath the trees were bushes so thickly woven together that you had to crawl on your hands and knees to get to the cool and shadowy secret places inside.

There were two children, a boy and a girl, and they lived with their father. They loved to play among the trees. Sometimes they heard the footfalls of animals they couldn't quite see because of all the leaves. Sometimes they lay in the shadows and watched their father at work on his lawn.

AS THE SUMMERS PASSED, the flowers on the trees would drop away and be followed by the appearance of seeds, and the seeds, which had tiny wings and sails, would blow onto the lawn of the house. And, later, some would sprout and begin to grow. But the children's father, who worked hard all day but liked to have his lawn look perfect, would go out in the evening and pluck out the sprouts or cut them down with his lawn mower. Trees are not so easily discouraged, however, and every summer they would send more seeds flying his way.

THIS WENT ON YEAR AFTER YEAR, and the children slowly grew up, as children will, and in time became a young man and a young woman, ready to go off into the world. By now they had gotten too big to crawl around in the trees and bushes next door, but sometimes they went and stood at their edge and remembered how much fun they'd had playing there when they were small.

Their father had grown older, too, but even though his back was stiff, he still fussed over his lawn, plucking out the sprouting trees as soon as they showed just one little leaf above the grass. The sweet smell of the little green flowers floated around him as he worked, but he was too busy to notice. It seemed that the older the children got, and the closer they were to leaving home for good, the harder their father worked on his lawn. And the winged seeds kept coming, and then the little sprouts came up, waving a leaf or two.

AND THEN THERE CAME A DAY when the children were gone for good and their father was living alone in the house with its perfect lawn all around. It's said that he began to feel that to keep up a house and yard was too much work for him now that he was getting older and his children were gone and he was alone, and at last he decided to sell the house and find an apartment in the city, maybe somewhere near his son and daughter. And maybe they'd invite him over for dinner once in a while.

Before long, he had moved away and there was a FOR SALE sign in the yard.
Around the sign's two legs, long grass was starting to grow, and here and
there on the lawn, little trees were sprouting—ash or elm or hackberry
or cottonwood—waving their bright leaves.

AS IT HAPPENED, nobody wanted to buy the house. Nobody could explain why, but it just didn't seem like a house where anybody wanted to live. That happens sometimes.

The paint on the house began to flake and peel, and some of the shingles blew off the roof. In the gutters along the edge of the roof, tiny trees sprouted. One evening, somebody threw a rock and broke one of the front windows, and within a few months, all the other windows had been broken out and sparrows were nesting inside. The FOR SALE sign fell over and nobody put it back.

NOW AND THEN the father would come to have a look at the house, hoping that maybe somebody had left a note saying they'd like to buy it, and he would prop up the sign one more time, and maybe he'd fix one of the windows, but no one ever left a note, and in a few more years, he quit coming back.

Some of the seeds had sprouted along the foundation, where water ran off the roof and into a deep crack, and these little trees were soon saplings, pressed against the side of the house.

When the wind blew, they waved back and forth, making dark arcs on the fading paint.

Where the shingles had blown away, the roof began to leak, and soon there were rotted places where the rain fell inside. When a roof goes bad, the rest of the house follows, and before long, the house was beginning to collapse, its nails rusting and pulling loose and its walls pulling apart at the corners.

The winds pushed at the house, but the young trees kept it from falling apart, and as they grew bigger and stronger, they held it together as if it was a bird's nest in the fingers of their branches.

And very gradually, the growing trees began to lift the house off its foundation.

First there was a crack of light beneath it, and then, in a few more years, you could see all the way across the top of the foundation.

THE TREES LIFTED IT AND LIFTED IT, and maybe you will drive past it today or tomorrow, as it floats there above the ground like a tree house, a house in the trees, a house held together by the strength of trees, and the wind blowing, perfumed by little green flowers.

To my granddaughters,
Margaret and Penelope Kooser
T. K.

For Dad
J. K.

Text copyright © 2012 by Ted Kooser
Illustrations copyright © 2012 by Jon Klassen

First edition 2012

Library of Congress Cataloging-in-Publication Data is available.
Library of Congress Catalog Card Number pending
ISBN 978-0-7636-5107-7

12 13 14 15 16 CCP 10 9 8 7 6 5 4 3 2

Printed in Shenzhen, Guangdong, China

This book was typeset in Mrs. Eaves.
The illustrations were created digitally and in gouache.

Candlewick Press
99 Dover Street
Somerville, Massachusetts 02144

visit us at www.candlewick.com